Naomi G. Sved is a therapy dog handler. Her previous publishing credits include, *Maggie the Therapy Dog*, a children's book which is based on her experiences with Maggie in the therapy world.

Naomi is also a contributor to *The Poet's Haven*, an online poetry forum.

Naomi is a mother of four, and a grandmother of six. She lives with her husband in Pennsylvania.

Dedicated to my sister, Ellen, who is always available to listen, encourage and understand me. I am so fortunate to have you in my life.

To my niece, Shani, who opened my eyes to the world of service dogs.

Naomi G. Sved

DIANA'S WISH

AUSTIN MACAULEY PUBLISHERS™

LONDON • CAMBRIDGE • NEW YORK • SHARJAH

Ordering Information
Quantity sales: Special discounts are available on quantity purchases by corporations, associations, and others. For details, contact the publisher at the address below.

Publisher's Cataloging-in-Publication data
Sved, Naomi G.
Diana's Wish

ISBN 9781649799951 (Paperback)
ISBN 9781649799968 (ePub e-book)

Library of Congress Control Number: 2022900779

www.austinmacauley.com/us

First Published 2022
Austin Macauley Publishers LLC
40 Wall Street, 33rd Floor, Suite 3302
New York, NY 10005
USA

mail-usa@austinmacauley.com
+1 (646) 5125767

In acknowledgment of all the hard workers raising and training service dogs, in an effort to ease the lives of those in need.

Chapter 1

October 9, 2014 was an ordinary day for most people. But not for me. I was in math class sitting next to my best friend, Keesha. One minute I was looking at an equation Mr. Ryan had written on the board.

$$130- \_\_\_ = 80$$

I was about to raise my hand to answer the question; math was an easy subject for me, but the next thing I knew, I was laying on the floor.

I remembered looking up at the ceiling and noticing that one of the light bulbs was out. *Funny*, I thought, *I hadn't noticed that during class*. Mr. Ryan was standing over me, asking if I was all right, and Keesha was holding my hand.

Keesha must have noticed that I wet my pants because she covered me with her sweatshirt. I knew she was my best friend because this was her favorite sweatshirt, the one she saved her allowance money from the chores she did in her house, helping out with her younger brother, and changing the cat litter. This sweatshirt never left her shoulders. It took her less than a second to lay it over me, to shield me from embarrassment.

They helped me sit up. I noticed the rest of the class staring, all twenty-two pairs of eyes on me.

"What happened?" I asked.

"Not sure. But you'll be fine," Mr. Ryan assured me. "Keesha, why don't you help Diana to the nurse's office so she can call her mom," he added.

I sat in the nurse's office, waiting for my mom to pick me up. How interesting that I was sitting here, since my mom is a nurse herself. I had never been to the school nurse before. Happy to say I had never been sick enough for a visit. I looked around. I read the signs on the wall.

Be a germ buster.

Make time for good health.

School nurses keep students healthy and safe.

Be kind to animals.

I really liked that one. I wondered who came up with the slogans. I also wondered if my mom had any of these signs in her office. I had to ask her.

I must have dozed because I awoke to voices. I could make out my mom's voice. It was mixed with sniffles, her way of trying to hold back from crying. I heard the concern in her words, but then again, she was always concerned. Keesha's mom said that's what happens when you're a single mom.

I tried to make out the conversation between my mom and the nurse, but I only heard bits and pieces. I decided to lie back down and wait.

Chapter 2

Mom kept talking as we drove to the pediatrician's office. I tried telling her I felt fine and just wanted to go home, but she wouldn't listen to me. Actually, what she said was:

"Since I already took the rest of the day off, we might as well get you checked out."

I tried talking her into taking me out for ice cream, but she said we would have to wait to hear what the doctor had to say first.

I found myself fingering the fabric of the sweat pants the nurse had given me as a replacement for the jeans I had ruined. I guess she kept extra in her office for times like these. I bounced back and forth between thinking there was something terribly wrong with me and thinking it would never happen again. I looked out the window and watched the houses go by. I never really paid attention to the scenery when I was sitting on the school bus. I was usually too busy talking to Keesha and my other friends. But now, I paid attention to the white houses with brown shutters. The leaves were starting to fall from the trees. I loved this time of year. Keesha and I always collected the leaves in her yard and then jumped in them for fun.

My mom called my name.

"Diana, Diana, you haven't heard a word I said. What are you daydreaming about?"

I turned to look at my mother. I noticed gray strands in her hair. *When did that creep up on her?*

"Mom, what's wrong with me?" I asked.

"I'm not sure," she responded. "But that's why it's important to get you checked out."

I nodded and turned my attention back to the emptying trees outside. Just like my insides. I forced myself to think of the Halloween party coming up at school. Mom promised we could go shopping this weekend for my costume. I hadn't decided yet what I wanted my costume to be, but I hoped she wouldn't change her mind. I really wanted to go to the mall.

We didn't have to wait long to see the doctor. There weren't too many sick kids at the doctor's office. The nurse handed me a paper robe and asked me to change. Ugh! I didn't like these gowns. They made me itchy. I put Keesha's sweatshirt over my shoulders because it was so cold in the office. Mom stayed with me while Dr. Wolf checked my eyes, ears, and nose. She looked in my mouth and asked me to say 'aahh.' She listened to my heart and took my blood pressure. She asked me to lie down and pressed on my stomach. I didn't really like that because I'm ticklish.

"I have the report from the school nurse, but why don't you tell me in your own words what happened," she said.

I looked at my mom, who nodded at me with reassurance.

"I don't know," I began. "One minute I was sitting at my desk looking at a math equation on the board, and the next minute I was on the floor. It happened so fast."

"Did anything hurt you this morning before you went to school?" Dr. Wolf asked.

I thought a minute and then shook my head no.

"How about now, does anything in particular hurt?" she added.

"No," I replied quickly while licking my lips. I guess I should have told her I was thirsty. I was getting bored with these questions and wanted to go for the ice cream.

"She wet her pants," my mom interjected.

"Mom!" I yelled out of embarrassment.

"Diana, Dr. Wolf needs to know everything."

"It's all right. All the information you tell me stays in this room. It's called doctor-patient confidentiality," Dr. Wolf added.

I lowered my eyes, not wanting to add anything to the conversation.

"I could send you for an EEG, but my guess is that you were simply dehydrated and a little low on sleep," Dr. Wolf continued.

"What's an EEG?" I questioned, my curiosity a little piqued.

"EEG stands for electroencephalogram. It's when a technician attaches electrodes to your scalp. It records your brain's electrical activity," Dr. Wolf said.

I must have made a face because Dr. Wolf added, "It doesn't hurt at all. But I don't think we're there yet. I do want to know if anything else unusual occurs. I want you to eat plenty of healthy foods, hydrate, and get a full night's sleep."

I nodded with a sigh of relief.

"Why don't you get dressed while I talk with your mom," Dr. Wolf said as she got up from the stool.

I watched my mom close the door and jumped off the examination table. I heard them talking in the hallway but couldn't make out what they were saying. I quickly dressed and opened the door. By then, Dr. Wolf was walking away, and Mom was checking her cell phone for messages.

"Ready for that ice cream?" she asked. I scanned her face to see if I could detect what she had discussed with the doctor, but she turned and walked away. I ran after her.

"Did Dr. Wolf say anything else?" I questioned, trying to look my mother in the eye as she continued to walk out to the car.

"Nothing for you to worry about," she answered.

I knew I wasn't going to get anything else out of her, so I let it go.

Chapter 3

We headed to the mall, to our favorite ice cream store. The place was empty. I had never been there in the middle of the week. I looked around and saw some elderly people walking in their workout shoes and a few mothers with their strollers, babies inside sleeping soundly.

We entered the ice cream store and saw our neighbor, Kenny, who was working the register. I said hi and went to check out the flavors. My mom took a few minutes and spoke with Kenny. She was like that, always concerned with what the kids in the neighborhood were doing. When she finished her conversation, she approached me.

"Decide on a flavor yet?"

"My usual, peanut butter mixed with banana. What about you?"

"I'll probably just go with a small cup of vanilla frozen yogurt. I got on the scale this morning and didn't like what I saw," my mom responded with a frown.

I swore when I got to be her age, I would never count my calories or watch what I ate. Why do adults worry so much? That's all my mom thinks about all day. I watch her measure her food on one of those food scales she leaves on the kitchen counter. I'm not sure it even helps.

After we ate, I tried to convince her to take me shopping for my Halloween costume. She wouldn't budge. She thought I had enough for one day. I didn't want to admit it, but she was probably right. I was feeling a little tired. By the time we got home, I was happy to lie on the sofa and watch TV. Our cat Clancy soon joined me, and before I knew it, I was fast asleep.

That night Keesha stopped by to pick up her sweatshirt. I was hoping she would let me keep it overnight because it was so comfortable, but when I heard the doorbell ring, I knew it had to be her. I was watching television when my mom answered the door. I heard her tell Keesha she would find me in the den.

"Hey, I brought you your homework. I knew you wouldn't want to fall behind in class," she said as I watched her eyes shift to her sweatshirt resting on my shoulders.

"Thanks," I said as I removed it and handed it to her. "I was going to bring your sweatshirt to school tomorrow."

"How do you feel?" she asked.

"All right, the doctor doesn't think it was anything too serious," I answered. "Mom took me out for ice cream. But I couldn't convince her to let me try on Halloween costumes."

"I'm glad you're feeling better. I have to go. My dad's waiting for me in the car. I'll see you tomorrow in school," Keesha said as she got up to go.

Keesha and I have known each other since we were three years old. Our mothers met while looking for daycare for us. They bumped into each other twice while checking out two different centers. They decided to get together for coffee so they could compare notes, figuring it was better to have two minds making a final decision. Eventually, they introduced us, and we became instant friends. We've been by each other's side ever since.

Chapter 4

The next day the whole school gathered for an assembly to discuss the details of the Halloween party. All kids in the middle school were talking at the same time. Principal White had to practically yell into the microphone to get everyone's attention.

"Boys, girls, I know you are excited, but if you don't let me speak, you won't hear the details, and we won't be able to get started."

Finally, the room quieted down, which wasn't easy for all of us. I looked around. There were still some girls giggling, but for the most part, everyone was quiet.

"Friday afternoon, October 31st," Principal White began, "we will be having a Halloween party. Our class parents have been gracious enough to organize a party for you. After our last period of the day, everyone will have a chance to change into their costumes. I will call you class by class to this very auditorium.

"We will have refreshments and music, with a few surprises as well. At some point in the afternoon, each class will be called to the stage to show off their costumes. Every class is going to be assigned a task to help their class parents. When you get back to your classroom, your teacher will go over the details. This is going to be a lot of fun, and I'm looking forward to it."

"Hey, Mr. White," a kid shouted from the back. "What's your costume going to be?"

"You'll have to wait and see!" Mr. White answered with a sly smile.

I grabbed Keesha's hand, and she squeezed back.

"We have to get to the mall this weekend and decide what our costumes will be," we both said at the same time.

"I'll work on my mom. Maybe she can drive us," I added as we got up and headed back to our classroom.

When everyone settled down, Mr. Ryan told us our class was assigned the decorations for the tables.

"Noah, why don't you come up to the board and write down the ideas as we talk about them? I'll copy them onto my computer." Mr. Ryan added.

The class as a whole decided on:

-Orange and black tablecloths
-Small pumpkins as centerpieces
-Confetti
-Streamers wrapped around the tables
-Cutouts of ghosts and goblins (the boys chose those)

The money to buy the decorations was coming from the PTO. Gabe and Annabelle said they would ask their mothers to buy the decorations.

The rest of the day was a blur. Everyone was so excited it was hard to pay attention to Mr. Ryan. As soon as the bell rang, we jumped out of our chairs, collected our backpacks, and headed for the bus. I couldn't wait to get home and talk to my mom about planning a trip to the mall with Keesha to buy our costumes.

Chapter 5

The day of the party, I woke up excited. I jumped out of bed, got dressed, and was downstairs before my mom. The night before, I had prepared my costume to bring to school; it was in a bag on the table. I looked it over, making sure I hadn't forgotten anything.

"Morning, pumpkin," Mom said as she came into the kitchen. "Did you eat anything yet?"

"No, I was just looking over my costume. I'm going to grab a bowl of cereal," I answered with a smile. After a quick breakfast, I grabbed my costume and said goodbye. I headed to the bus stop. I couldn't remember being so excited about going to school. I was a good student and liked school, but this was different. Today wasn't about learning; it was more like a fun day.

In math class, we were learning double-digit subtraction, which I had already mastered. In English, we broke up into small groups and practiced our reading skills. I'm in the highest group. Our last class of the day, Social Studies, is the class I like the least. I get bored learning about the American presidents. Mom says I can grow up to be president one day, but I already know I want to be a mathematician. The STEM program was just introduced into our school this year, and I am hoping to go to the summer program.

Finally, the bell rang. Everyone jumped out of their seats and cheered. Our teacher had to shout to get our attention.

"Boys and girls, settle down! Everyone will have a chance to change into their costumes. Girls, you may take your costumes and head to the bathroom. Boys, please stay here and change into your costumes."

We practically ran down the hallway with our costumes in our hands. When we entered the bathroom, there were so many girls we had to wait our turn until we could find room for ourselves. After a few minutes, the bathroom emptied out. We helped each other with zippers, buttons, hats, and sashes. Some of us had makeup to put on, while others wore more simple costumes. When we finished changing, I looked around. I saw two of my friends dressed as Wonder Woman, one doctor, one nurse, one cowgirl, and one firefighter. Keesha and I had decided to be two different colors of crayons. I was my favorite color purple and Keesha was hers, red. Everyone shrieked with delight.

We headed back to the classroom. We joined the boys who had already changed into their costumes. Mr. Ryan had us line up by the door. We waited to hear from the principal so we could start the procession to the auditorium.

When we finally got the word to go, the hallway filled up quickly. Mr. Ryan insisted we walk in a straight line to the auditorium. Some of the other classes walked like us, but there were kids running down the hall. Mr. Ryan had to remind them to slow down. I felt excitement in the air. When the doors opened, the music made my ears tingle. I felt a little strange. My body didn't move like it was supposed to; I was dizzy.

When we saw Mr. White dressed as a zombie, Keesha and I giggled. It was the funniest sight we had ever seen.

Keesha grabbed my hand, and we raced around the room, looking at all the decorations and the refreshments. We made a plan. We would have some punch, then dance, and return to the refreshments for some pumpkin-flavored donuts. We would take our turn at the pin the tail on the goblin. It was going to be a great afternoon.

The music was so loud that at times it was hard to hear what Keesha was saying. Luckily she kept hold of my hand and dragged me across the room. When I asked her if she thought the punch tasted funny, she looked at me and shrugged her shoulders. She grabbed my hand again, and we raced to the apple bobbing station. We decided not to try this because we didn't want to get our costumes wet. But it was fun watching the boys sticking their heads in the water and try to grab the apples with their mouths.

By the time we headed for the donuts, my head was hurting. I didn't want to tell anyone, because I didn't want to miss out on any fun. I knew they would insist I go to the nurse's office.

My head didn't feel any better after eating the donut. Keesha kept asking me what was wrong, because I kept rubbing my head, but I told her nothing was wrong.

Mr. Ryan had a hard time calling us together because it was close to the time for the procession on the stage. By this time, my head was pounding so hard I could hardly see straight. I forced a smile on my face as we walked up the stairs, but I really wanted to go home. The pounding in my head wouldn't go away. As we walked across the stage, I saw white spots in my eyes, and the next thing I knew, I crumbled to the floor.

Chapter 6

The noise was bothering me, but nothing I did could make it stop. I turned my head to the left, still heard the noise. I turned my head to the right, still heard the noise. I tried covering my ears with my hands. That's when I heard a voice I didn't recognize.

"She's awake. Diana, how are you feeling?" someone asked me.

Why does everyone keep asking me the same question? I thought as I opened my eyes. I looked around and didn't recognize anything, especially the face staring down at me. I bolted up, nearly colliding heads with this stranger.

"Whoa, take it easy. Everything's all right. You're all right. You're in an ambulance. You passed out at your school party. We are on the way to the hospital. Your mom is meeting us there," this stranger explained.

I continued to stare and then noticed a tube attached to my arm.

"Don't be concerned about that," this stranger said when he noticed me poking at the tube. "That's an intravenous line giving you fluids to hydrate you."

"What's that?" I pointed to a machine that was making a beeping noise.

"That's monitoring your heart rate," he answered, "and right now, it's above normal. Why don't you lie back down until we get to the hospital? We're almost there."

I didn't understand what elevated meant, but I guess it wasn't good, so I lay back down. I was so tired from running around the party with Keesha, and the beeping was hurting my head. I knew my mom would be freaked out when she saw me like this. I just wanted to close my eyes and start the day over.

I kept my eyes closed as I was taken out of the ambulance. I didn't want to look at all the faces staring at me. They took me to a small cubicle and told me my mom was on the way. A few minutes later, I heard her asking where I was. The curtain was pushed aside, and she rushed in. I could tell she had been crying.

"I'm fine," I said.

"Has anyone been in to see you yet?" she questioned.

"No, we just got here. The man from the ambulance said the doctor would be here in a minute," I assured her.

"Hi, I'm Dr. Coleman. I understand Diana had a little incident at school today."

"Yes, and she passed out last week as well. Her pediatrician Dr. Wolf has been monitoring her," my mom explained.

I lay back and let my mom and the doctor talk for a bit. I had no interest in getting involved with this discussion. I could tell my mom was upset, her hands were clenched, and she dismissed the doctor's offer for her to sit down.

So, this is serious, I thought. *Not good at all.*

After a few minutes, my mom came over, patted me on the head, and smiled.

Really?! Now she was treating me like a baby.

"Diana, they've decided to admit you so they can observe you and run some tests," my mom explained.

"What about Halloween? What about all the plans Keesha and I have?" I shouted, but at the same time, I had this nagging feeling at the back of my mind that this time I should just let it go.

"Diana, you know your health is more important than anything. Let's get everything figured out, then get back to your plans," Mom patted my shoulder, trying to soothe me.

Even that small gesture bothered me. I refused to let her see me cry. One of us had to be the brave one.

Chapter 7

After I was settled in my room (at least no old person for a roommate), my mom said she was going to check out the cafeteria for a snack. I kept telling her I wasn't hungry, so I figured it had to be for her. She always was a nervous eater.

I must have dozed (why do I keep doing this?), because all of a sudden, I smelled something familiar. At first, I couldn't put my finger on it. Then I opened my eyes. My grandmother was sitting in the room. The scent I was smelling was her perfume. I turned to my right, and my grandfather winked at me.

"Hey, kiddo, you didn't have to pass out for us to visit," he said jokingly.

I smiled.

"There's that smile I love to see," he said as both my grandparents came to the side of my bed.

"Your mom went home to get some clothes. She figured you'd want to change out of your costume," my grandmother added.

I looked down, and for the first time since arriving at the hospital, I realized I was still in my purple crayon costume.

"I like your costume," my grandfather said as he sat on the corner of the bed.

"Keesha is the red crayon," I answered, smoothing out the fabric of my costume. "Do you think I'll get to go trick-or-treating?" I asked.

"Well, kiddo, that's up to your mom and the docs. Why don't we wait to see what they have to say? It's more important to get you all fixed up. Don't you agree?" my grandfather asked with half a smile.

I didn't have time to answer; at that moment, my mom returned with a bag slung over her shoulders. She started to tell me what she packed for me when a nurse walked into the room and said I needed to change into a hospital gown. She was taking me for an EEG followed by an MRI.

"Best to get both done and the results in as quickly as possible," she said.

I didn't have to ask what an EEG was. Dr. Wolf had explained it when I was in her office. I took the gown and headed for the bathroom when I heard my mom say, "Are both of these tests really necessary?"

"The neurologist thinks so," the nurse replied.

"Do you need any help changing?" my mom called out to me.

"No, I got this," I answered.

When I finished changing, there was a wheelchair waiting for me.

"Really!" I said, rolling my eyes. "This is a little too much. Why do I need that?"

"Hospital rules," the nurse explained. "Mom, why don't you come with us? Grandma and Grandpa can wait here. It shouldn't take too long," she continued.

I listened to my mom and nurse chat as we weaved through the halls of the hospital. The corridors were filled with doctors and people who nodded at us as we passed them.

"We're here," the nurse said as she hit a large silver button on a wall with the word RADIOLOGY written on it.

As we entered, I looked around. It wasn't what I had expected. The room was quiet. It was a nice change after all the noise from the main hospital. We were met by a young man who wore the same white uniform, but his said TECHNICIAN on it. I didn't understand what that word meant, but I figured I would look it up on my computer when I got home.

When we got back to my room, my grandfather was stretched out on my bed, fiddling with the remote control for the television, and my grandmother was dozing on the only chair on my side of the room. In her hand were two Mylar balloons with the words 'Get Well Soon.'

"Oh, hey, kiddo, back so soon," my grandfather said with a smile.

"Anything good on TV?" I questioned, deciding to play along with this game everyone is playing, not talking about what is really going on.

"Just checking it out for you," he answered while he continued playing with the remote.

"Dad," my mom said, "time to let Diana have her bed back."

"Oh, sure, sorry, got distracted for a minute, kiddo," he added with a wink.

I climbed out of the wheelchair and into the bed.

"Mom, did you bring me my favorite socks, the ones with the pink bows on them?"

"Sure did," she answered as she dug into the bag that was sitting on the window sill.

"I also brought your favorite photo," she said, handing me the picture I keep on my dresser at home. I looked at the picture of my father holding me when I was a baby. I have no memory of it, but strangely it gives me comfort. Maybe because today I can tell I look like him. My mom told me this was before he became sick. It was a quick illness, cancer. Not that he was sick for very long. Sometimes cancer is like that. We don't talk about it much. It makes her sad. But every once in a while, I catch her looking at old photos. I see her smile. I know she was happy back then. But when the tears start to flow, I watch her put the pictures away.

I put on my socks and got comfortable, and asked my mom the time. When she told me 4:30, I knew school was over, and the Halloween party was finished. I wondered if Keesha and the rest of the gang forgot about me after the ambulance pulled away. I could envision the race to get ready to go trick-or-treating in my neighborhood. *Did all my friends stop at my house?* My poor sweet cat, Clancy. He'd be so confused every time the doorbell rang, and we weren't there to open it.

My grandmother woke up and handed me the balloons with a kiss on my forehead.

"Here, honey. I thought this would brighten up the room."

"Thanks," I murmured without even glancing at them.

I noticed a look pass between my mother and my grandmother.

"Come, Nate, it's time to let Diana rest," my grandmother called to my grandfather.

With a wink and a kiss, they were out the door.

I picked up the remote and played with it for a few minutes while my mom pulled out my favorite blanket she brought and covered the bed in an attempt to make me feel at home.

"I grabbed the book that was sitting on your nightstand," she said as she handed me a paperback I had been reading at night before going to sleep. I was halfway through the book.

I looked at the book, one I had borrowed from our local library, and said, "I don't plan on finishing it while I'm here."

My mom set herself up for the night on the chair in my room, saying she didn't want to leave me alone. The doctors had told us they would have the results of the EEG and MRI first thing in the morning. They felt it best to have me stay overnight for observation.

Observation! I didn't like that word. What did it mean anyway? Was someone going to stand over me and watch me while I slept? My mom being a nurse, agreed with the doctors.

"It's only for one night," she said. "Besides, I'll keep you company. Think of it as a slumber party."

I rolled my eyes and played with the buttons that moved the bed…up and down, up and down.

I watched a little television while my mom checked her emails. We played some card games she brought from home, and by 9 o'clock, we turned off the lights and went to sleep.

Sometime in the middle of the night, I woke up. It took me a minute to remember I was in the hospital. I heard my mom breathing softly and knew she was sound asleep. I lay awake for a while but finally decided to get up and go for a walk. I unhooked the wires from my arms and placed them gently on my bed, hoping it wouldn't set off any alarms. My room wasn't far from the nurse's station. A few of the nurses were talking with each other. As I got closer, I saw a flashing red light near the desk. I stopped in my tracks and watched it flash on and off. For some reason, I couldn't take my eyes off of it. I saw one of the nurses turn to me. At first, she smiled, but I saw her expression change. The next thing I remember, the nurse is looking over me calling my name. I open my eyes and feel the cold floor under me.

Chapter 8

I've been home a month now. My mother watches me like a hawk, and when she goes to work, my grandparents stay with me. After passing out at the hospital, the doctors were finally able to figure out what is wrong with me. They call it a seizure disorder. My brain is sending mixed signals, so it shuts down. That's why I pass out. I've been put on medicine, lots of it, and because of that, I haven't been able to go back to school. I miss my friends and don't like being stuck at home. Once a week, my mom goes to my school and picks up all of my work, so I don't fall behind, but the medicine makes me sleepy, so I don't feel like doing work most of the time.

Keesha stopped by twice and told me all about what's been happening at school.

"Nobody took over your desk," she told me, "we all expect you to come back." I hope Keesha didn't notice me wipe the tears from my eyes. "The class is getting ready for the Thanksgiving play," she continued.

I had forgotten about the play and didn't even remember Thanksgiving was coming up. Nobody in my family has been talking about it.

The next time Keesha came to hang out, it was a Saturday afternoon after Keesha finished her basketball practice. Mom was out doing errands with Grandma, and Grandpa was changing lightbulbs around the house. Keesha and I were listening to music I had on my computer. It was good to see Keesha. I missed hanging with her and the rest of the kids at school. Keesha told me about a new boy that had transferred into our class. His family came from Memphis. He has a funny accent, she told me, but I could tell she liked him. She had this half-smile she always had when she talked about something she liked.

Wow, I thought. *First, I'm missing out on the Thanksgiving play, and now I'm missing out on Keesha's first crush.*

After Keesha left, my grandfather found me in my room.

"Hey, kiddo, want some ice cream?" he handed me a bowl of peanut butter crunch.

As I took the bowl, Clancy meowed and crawled onto my bed. My grandfather pulled up a chair, and we sat quietly, eating our ice cream.

"Want to talk about it?" he asked after we finished our ice cream.

"Talk about what?" I asked.

My grandfather didn't answer, just raised his eyebrows. I took my finger and drew circles with the melted ice cream in my bowl.

"It's not fair," I began. "Everyone's life is going on, and I'm stuck here. I feel forgotten. It's been a month. The

35

doctor's said I would be better by now. So, why aren't I allowed to go back to school?"

I felt my grandfather's eyes on me while I played with Clancy's fur.

"Why don't I talk to your mom and see about the two of you going to school for the Thanksgiving play?" he said.

I lifted my head, and our eyes met.

"There's the twinkle I've been missing," he added.

I climbed off my bed and gave him a hug.

"Thanks, Grandpa, you're the best!"

"Well, it's not a done deal. Let me see if I can work my magic," he said with a wink.

Chapter 9

I was a little nervous but happy a week later as Mom and I drove to school to see the Thanksgiving play. It hadn't been too hard convincing her to let me go. My grandfather's magic had worked. First, I had a follow-up appointment at the doctor's, my neurologist. I wasn't as sleepy during the day, I told him, and my seizures were down to once every two days. The meds were starting to kick in.

I was nervous because other than seeing Keesha twice, I hadn't seen or heard from the rest of my class. What would they think of me? It would be weird watching the play and not being a part of it. But, at the same time, I was happy to be out of the house. Mom told me Keesha's family had invited us (even Grandma and Grandpa) to their house for Thanksgiving dinner. That would be twice in one week I would have somewhere to go.

"I want to bake a pie. Should I make apple or pecan?" Mom asked.

Mom looked over at me.

"Diana, you're not answering me!"

"What?" I asked as I pulled my eyes off the empty trees. *When did this happen?* The last time I was on the bus looking at the trees, they still had some leaves left on their limbs. It felt like ages ago.

"I said what pie should I bake to take to Keesha's house, apple or pecan?"

"Why not both?" I answered.

"Hmm," my mom said.

The play was great! It was a comedy of the Pilgrims and the Indians sharing a Thanksgiving meal. We were laughing the whole time. I was happy to sit in the back row with my mom. That was until Mr. White, the principal, pointed me out and welcomed me. Everyone turned around and stared. I was so embarrassed, if only the floor would open up and swallow me. My mom grabbed my hand and squeezed it.

When the play was over, Mom encouraged me to find my friends. Keesha saw me approaching. She ran and gave me a big hug. Together we walked back to the rest of the group.

"Hey, everyone," I said. "Great job."

"Thanks," the class responded without much enthusiasm.

We stood staring at each other, not knowing what to say.

Keesha broke the ice.

"Diana's feeling better and is hoping to come back to school soon, right, Diana?" Keesha said with a forced smile as she looked at me.

Tears welled up in my eyes. *Don't cry; don't cry*, I told myself as I looked at the ground. When I forced myself to bring my head up, everyone around me was looking at their feet.

"Well, I gotta go," I said when I finally found my voice. "Bye, everyone," I muttered as I turned around and headed back to where my mom was waiting for me. As I approached her, I saw she was talking with Keesha's mom.

"We're so happy you're joining us for Thanksgiving dinner, Diana," Keesha's mom said.

"Mom, can we go, please!" I said.

"Diana, don't be rude. Someone said something to you, and you didn't respond," my mom said, glaring at me.

"Mom, I need to go now," I repeated. I turned to walk away as I heard my mom say something about hormones.

Driving home, my mom started in on me about my manners. I sat staring out the window, silent.

"Diana," my mom finally stopped talking. "What's wrong?"

"You don't get it," I started talking as I felt tears roll down my cheeks.

"Everyone treats me differently. They could hardly look at me, and when they do, they don't know what to say. Going to the play was a big mistake!"

Chapter 10

During Thanksgiving dinner, Keesha kept telling me stories about what's going on in school. She was sitting on my right, with my mother on my left. My grandparents were across the table from me. They were part of the adult conversation, which I had no interest in being a part of. Once in a while, I would look over at my grandfather, and he would give me his crooked smile accompanied by his requisite wink. I smiled back and turned my attention to Keesha.

Keesha continued to tell me which kids were hanging out with each other and the latest clicks that were forming. As much as I missed being in school, it was something I really didn't want to be a part of.

The food was amazing, and there was so much of it. Keesha's dad cooked the turkey, and he kept insisting when the wishbone was uncovered, Keesha and I had a claim to it.

We were to make a wish and break it. A tradition in their home, something I didn't quite understand but was willing to try. I already knew what my wish would be.

Terrence, Keesha's little brother, was not too happy about it.

"Hey, that's my job," he protested.

"Diana is our guest," Keesha's mom said. "Why not let her give it a try this year?"

Poor Terrence. He pouted the rest of the meal.

In the end, Mom had baked two pies: apple and pecan. Pecan was my favorite, so I made sure to leave room for dessert. Grandma brought flowers for the centerpiece, and Grandpa had insisted on stopping at the store on the way over and picking up vanilla ice cream.

"Who serves apple pie without vanilla ice cream?" he said at least five times on the car ride over. It made Mom bonkers, so she finally found a grocery store that was open, and Grandpa bought two containers.

When dinner was over, we all got up to help clear the dishes and bring out the dessert. That's when Keesha's uncle approached me.

"So I hear you have seizures," he said.

I felt my face go red.

Keesha's mom came to my rescue as she said, "Isaiah, maybe Diana doesn't want to talk about it right now."

"I train service dogs," he continued.

I had no idea what that meant, so I just shifted my eyes and looked at my shoes.

"Oh, we have them, and their handlers come through the hospital," my mom said.

"You must mean therapy dogs," Isaiah said. "There's a big difference between a therapy dog and a service dog. A therapy dog is one that offers comfort to someone, and a service dog helps people navigate through society."

I started listening to the conversation between my mom and Keesha's uncle without really understanding what they were saying. Keesha had never told me what her uncle did for a living.

"Most of the service dogs we train are Labrador Retrievers that live with trained individuals from the time they are puppies. They are raised in a household that is approved, and the puppies go to special classes. When they reach a certain age, they are tested to see if they qualify for additional training to be a service dog for people that are blind, wheelchair-bound people, people with seizures or other disabilities."

I was so in tune with my cat Clancy that I never knew a dog had the ability to be a service dog.

My mom and Keesha's uncle moved their conversation back to the table as we finished clearing and got out the dessert.

My mom's pies were a hit, as well as the vanilla ice cream that my grandpa happily took credit for. Keesha's mom insisted we let them finish the cleanup.

As we headed home, I asked my mom what she thought about the service dog.

"It's an interesting concept, but I don't think it's for us," she said.

"Why not?" I asked.

"Well, for one, we don't know the first thing about dogs," she began, "and secondly, it's a big responsibility."

"Oh," was the only thing I could think to say.

We dropped my grandparents off at their home.

"Think positively," my grandpa said as he got out of the car. My grandma waved and threw me a kiss.

We drove the rest of the way home, both lost in our own thoughts.

Chapter 11

It rained all weekend. I didn't have to look outside to feel the gloom. I felt the same. I spent all weekend on my iPad googling service dogs and therapy dogs. There was a lot of information. Why didn't I know about this? My neighbors had a dog. I heard them every so often playing fetch with her in their backyard, but I didn't even pay attention to them.

The therapy dogs online were all cute and cuddly, while the service dogs, who were still cute, were more serious. I didn't see any service dogs matched with young kids. Could I be the first? And why had my grandfather told me to think positively?

Most of the service dogs I saw were walking next to people in wheelchairs or with people who were walking with canes used for the blind. I saw service dogs opening refrigerators doors, picking objects off the floor, and even helping people retrieve change at a store. But these were things I didn't need. First of all, I was way too young, and second of all, when the time came, I could certainly do these things for myself.

I decided to google service dogs + seizure disorder. Bingo! A whole new thread of videos popped up, some even with explanations.

I read that service dogs are taught to detect a scent that comes before a seizure, lets its owner know, and gets them to a safe environment. Then I clicked on a video and watched as a dog nudged its owner, who then lay on the floor. As a seizure took over, the dog lay its head on the person's chest until it was over.

I was mesmerized. I had never seen myself when I had a seizure, and I was totally amazed how this dog learned how to detect an oncoming one and then protect its owner.

Clancy must have heard the videos because he appeared out of nowhere and jumped on my lap.

"No worries, Clancy, no matter what happens, you'll always come first," I said as I proceeded to pet him.

Then I looked at him. Animals must really have a sixth sense and understand when humans need them. I scampered off my bed and grabbed a treat from a bag I always kept on my desk. Clancy happily took it from my outstretched hand.

Chapter 12

At my next doctor's visit, I half-listened as my mom and Dr. Wolf discussed the possibility of my return to school, at least part-time. Winter break was fast approaching, and my days were running one into the other. I sat there thinking the break used to be called Christmas vacation, but over time was changed.

"The vacation needs to include everyone," our teachers explained. "Jamal celebrates Kwanza, Rebecca celebrates Hanukah, and Joseph is a Seventh-day Adventist, so he doesn't celebrate Christmas at all, and that's just in our class." So the words were changed to winter break.

I thought of the small Christmas tree we usually put up and knew we couldn't add any poinsettia plants because they are poisonous to Clancy.

"Diana, Diana. Where are you?" my mother said. "Always off in your own world. Could that be the effect of the meds?" she asked Dr. Wolf.

"I think she's just missing interaction with her peers," Dr. Wolf replied.

"Diana, we are talking about the possibility of getting you back to school part-time. What do you think about it?" Dr. Wolf asked me.

I hesitated in my response. On one hand, I was eager to get back to school, back to my friends, back to my routine. But would the kids accept me, or would they look at me like a freak? It's only been a few weeks since the Thanksgiving play, and it was a total disaster.

I looked at both Dr. Wolf and my mom and said, "I'm not sure."

Chapter 13

The day before Christmas, Mom and I were baking chocolate chip cookies in the kitchen.

"Grandma and Grandpa are on their way over," Mom said. "As soon as the cookies come out of the oven, Grandpa wants to take you on your traditional outing."

Every year, on Christmas Eve day, Grandpa and I drive around my neighborhood, looking at all the houses decked out in decorations. Although it isn't nighttime, we still enjoy seeing all the Santa and the reindeers set up in people's yards. I especially like the blow up decorations.

As the last batch of cookies came out of the oven, the front door opened.

"Something smells good," Grandpa said.

"You can take a few for the road, but we need to save the rest. I want to run a batch to my patients at the hospital," Mom said.

I grabbed my coat as Grandpa munched on a few cookies, and we headed to the door.

"No hug for me?" Grandma asked.

"Sorry, Grandma. I was so excited to have somewhere to go," I said as I walked back to give her a hug.

Finally, something fun to do, I thought. I looked forward to this tradition with my grandfather all year.

"See you all soon," I said to both my mom and grandma.

Grandpa and I climbed into his car. He looked at me, smiled, and gave me his customary wink. I put my seatbelt on and felt a chill go down my spine. Grandpa was up to something; I knew him well enough to know when he had something up his sleeve. I looked at his profile and noticed the smile on his face. *Guess I'll find out soon enough,* I thought, as I turned my attention to the road and noticed we had already driven out of my neighborhood.

"Grandpa, where are we going?" I asked.

He turned to me and said, "You'll see."

Well, I was out of the house, the sun was shining, and I was with my favorite grandpa. This should be interesting.

Fifteen minutes later, we pulled into a parking lot. I looked around. The lot was nearly empty. The red brick building looked old and sad. The sign on the front read GUIDE DOG SOCIETY. The look of confusion on my face prompted my grandfather to say, "Come on, you'll understand when we go inside."

The minute we opened the door, I heard barking. But it wasn't the kind of barking I heard at my neighbor's yard, the one from the small dog who kept at it until it was annoying. This barking was once. It stopped, and then I heard someone say a word, just like a command, but I didn't catch what was said. Then the dog barked again.

Isaiah, Keesha's uncle appeared.

"Hi, Diana, hi, Grandpa, nice to see you again."

My face must have registered shock because he turned to Grandpa and said, "Guess you didn't explain the reason for your visit."

"Diana," My grandfather said. "Isaiah invited us to his center to observe the training of the service dogs. He thought you might be interested in seeing the process and maybe meeting one of the dogs after their class."

"Does Mom know I'm here?"

"Yes," Grandpa answered. "She didn't have any objections."

Isaiah led us through the doors into the inner sanctuary, as he called it. As we walked, he told us that each dog sleeps at home with its master. They come to the center to learn tasks, like going to school. We stopped at a large window overlooking an indoor gym.

I watched four dogs on leashes standing by their master's side. A single trainer stood in front of each one of them at a time. He gave a command, and each master followed in turn. As the dog listened to its master, a treat was given to the dog. Peter explained this was training with positive reinforcement.

"What kind of dogs are these?" my grandfather asked.

"Labrador retrievers," Isaiah answered. "They are the best type of dogs for service dogs. They are easy to train and get along great with all types of people."

"How long has the program been in existence?" my grandfather asked another question.

"I've been running it just about five years now. I took it over from someone that moved out west. From what I understand, she had been running it for three years."

I half-listened to the conversation. I was more interested in watching what the dogs were doing, or better yet, what they were learning.

"What's with the dog sitting on the floor in the far corner?" I asked.

"Oh, that's Dino, he's my dog, a retired service dog," Isaiah responded.

"Why is he retired?" I asked.

"He developed cataracts and arthritis, and it was affecting his ability to help his master."

"So why do you have him?"

"They reached out to me because I trained him, and they wanted a good home for him. I decided to keep him myself. I knew I could bring him with me to the center every day."

After the session was over, Isaiah let us meet the dogs and the handlers. We were introduced to Jake, Kyle, Layla, and Maggie. We were told each litter is named by a letter of the alphabet. Since we are meeting Maggie, it means the breeder is halfway through the alphabet.

After instruction, the dogs are allowed playtime. They are let off the leash and roam around the gym, smelling and chasing each other.

"What are they doing?" I asked when I saw one dog smelling the butt of another dog.

"That's how dogs get to know each other, just like people shake hands," Isaiah explained.

All of a sudden, Dino started barking. He got up, moved closer to us, and ran around in circles.

"What's he doing now?" my grandfather asked.

Isaiah turned and gave me a funny look.

"Diana, how are you feeling? Did you take your meds this morning?"

I looked at him, looked at Dino, but before I could answer, felt myself crumple to the floor.

Chapter 14

I felt something heavy on my chest, and I was beginning to be aware of people talking around me. Someone was panting in my face. *Ugh, really bad breath*, I thought.

I opened my eyes and saw Dino staring at me. His paws were resting on my chest. I tried to sit up, but he wouldn't let me. Isaiah gave him a command, and he moved off of me. Grandpa helped me sit up. The concern I saw in his eyes frightened me. I'm not sure he had ever seen one of my seizures.

"I'm fine," I reassured him. I was hoping he would give me his crooked smile and his usual 'sure, kiddo,' but it did not come.

"Should I call an ambulance?" Isaiah asked.

"No, I'm fine," I repeated.

I looked at my grandfather and could tell he was trying to decide what to do. I knew I had to distract him.

"I thought you said Dino was retired?" I said, turning my attention to Isaiah.

"He is, but he obviously still has the skills he learned as a pup. He knew to warn you that a seizure was coming. He was trying to tell you to get down on the ground so you wouldn't be hurt."

I knelt down and wrapped my arms around Dino. His fur was soft and snuggly. Not much different than Clancy's.

"Time to get you home," Grandpa said, turning toward me. "Thanks, Isaiah, this is more than we could have imagined."

"Come back and visit anytime."

Grandpa put his arm around me and walked me back to the car. He helped me with my seatbelt. I knew not to complain, knew he needed to feel in control of the situation. I would let my mom explain to him that this was not his fault; my seizures just happen whenever they did.

"I never saw an actual seizure," Grandpa said.

"Neither did I," I said.

Grandpa looked at me and gave me his signature smile.

"Seriously," he continued. "Your whole body was shaking. I kept calling your name, but you didn't respond."

I looked at Grandpa, ready to respond but changed my mind. Nothing I said would make him feel any better.

I leaned my head back and must have fallen asleep because I felt the car shut off. I opened my eyes and saw my house in front of me. Mom was coming out of the front door, so I knew Isaiah had called to let her know what happened. I forced a smile on my face so she would know I was fine. Grandpa, on the other hand, I wasn't so sure about.

When I went into the house, Mom had my milk and cookies waiting for me. This had become a habit for us. She said there was no medical evidence that this helped after a seizure, but Mom needed to feel like she was doing something. Milk and cookies couldn't hurt, and besides, who doesn't like a good chocolate chip cookie dipped into a nutritious cup of milk.

It felt good to be home, in the comfort of my surroundings. Clancy heard us and climbed into my lap. He must have sensed I needed comforting.

I listened to my mom and Grandpa talking at the door.

"You should have seen Dino," my grandfather said. "He sprang right into action. I think you need to reconsider this as an option for Diana."

"I'm still working on getting her better," Mom replied. "The service dog comes later. I don't even think I can afford it."

"I've done some research," my grandpa added. "Lots of people set up these Go Fund Me pages. Why can't we do that?"

"You're not listening to me. Right now, I think the important thing is to get her meds straight, not worry about a service dog."

"What if they never get her meds right? Didn't you tell me they said there is always a chance she will have to live with this condition the rest of her life?"

"What?" I screamed. "You lied to me."

Mom and Grandpa turned to look at me. Clancy jumped out of my lap as I got up and ran to my room.

I heard the front door close, and a minute later, there was a knock on my door. Mom poked her head in.

"Can I come in?" she asked.

"Whatever," I said without looking at her.

"Diana, I know you're upset, but I didn't lie to you. The doctors are still figuring things out. Unfortunately, it takes time," my mother said.

"I'm tired of you telling me the same thing all the time."

"I know this is hard to understand, but sometimes doctors don't have all the answers."

I didn't say anything. There wasn't anything to say.

"I think it's about time you become involved in your medical plan. What do you think?" my mom asked.

I still didn't say anything.

My mom scrolled through her phone.

"Your next appointment is on Thursday after New Year's Day. Why don't we tell the doctor you want to be part of the discussion and decision from now on?"

I raised my head and looked at my mom.

"You really mean it?"

"Yes, but this doesn't mean you have the final say. It just means you can share your opinion and be PART of the decision process."

"What about the idea of a service dog?"

"We can raise that topic with the doctor if you'd like."

Clancy poked his head in my room, hesitated as if to ask, is it okay to come in? I jumped off my bed, scooped him up, and buried my face in his soft fur.

Chapter 15

On New Year's Eve, Keesha and I had a slumber party. Mom insisted we have it at our house, and I didn't mind at all. Keesha told me her parents were having a party at her house, and I wasn't in the mood to be around so many people. Mom ordered pizza and we made ice cream sundaes. Keesha and I got into our pajamas early and set up our sleeping bags in the den so we could get cozy in front of the big TV screen. We planned on staying up till midnight. Our goal was to be awake for the first of the New Year.

Around 9 o'clock, the doorbell rang. Mom opened the door, and we heard Grandma and Grandpa's voices. A few minutes later, Grandpa popped his head in the den and wished us a happy new year.

"What are you girls up to?" he asked.

"We're watching all the people on TV in New York City getting ready to celebrate the New Years," I said.

"Well, have fun. Grandma and I are on our way to a party and wanted to stop in to say hello," he said as he bent down to kiss me on my head. He threw a kiss to Keesha as he turned and left the room.

I heard the front door close, and Mom poked her head in to see if there was anything she could get us. She sat with us for a few minutes and then the doorbell rang again. The three of us looked at each other.

"Well, this is certainly a busy night," Mom said as she got up to answer the door.

"Isaiah, so nice to see you," Mom said. Keesha and I looked at each other. *Is something going on between my mom and Isaiah?*

Dino came barreling into the den.

"Dino," we yelled as we jumped up to hug him.

We settled Dino between us and turned our attention back to the TV.

We got up and started dancing when one of our favorite artists came on. Dino sat there watching us move about the room. We held our fists up as if they were microphones and sang the words to our favorite songs. It was just like the way I remember us hanging out before I got sick. When we got tired of dancing, we decided to look in on my mom and Isaiah to see what they were doing.

I looked at Dino and he looked back at me.

"Just give him the command of 'stay'," Keesha said.

So I said 'stay' and Dino didn't get up as we walked out of the room.

"How do you know so much about dogs?" I asked.

"Sometimes I go with my uncle to the center. I love hanging with the dogs and watching the training."

As we headed to the living room, I put my hand on Keesha's arm and she stopped in her tracks. We saw Isaiah and my mom sitting on the sofa looking at an iPad. They were concentrating on what was on the screen. I wondered what they were talking about.

"Ellen, I know you didn't ask me to open a 'Go Fund Me' page, your dad did. But in only a few days we've raised $5,000 toward a service dog for Diana. We're almost to our goal."

When I heard Isaiah say that, tears came to my eyes. Keesha hugged me. "Your dream is about to come true," she whispered in my ear.

"But I don't understand. How could this have happened? Who would have given us this money, and how does this even work?" my mom said.

"Don't worry so much, Ellen. I'm here to help. I'll take care of the logistics. You can thank everyone when it's all done."

I didn't hear my mom respond, so I peeked around the corner and saw her sitting with her head in her hands. I noticed a tear slide down her cheek. I know how hard this has been for her. She didn't have to tell me she thinks this is her fault. But I know it's not. It's just bad luck.

When she looked up, our eyes locked. She motioned for me to come to her. I climbed into her lap, and she wrapped her arms around me, something we haven't done since I was a little girl.

After Isaiah left, the three of us watched the ball drop at midnight. It was the first time I had stayed up so late. It was a night I would always remember.

Chapter 16

3 Months Later

The cold weather has gone, and the trees once again have green leaves. Grandpa takes me to and from school every day. I turn around in the car and in the backseat is Jake, my service dog. The township hasn't approved a dog riding the bus, but I'm not complaining. I like the time I get to spend with Grandpa.

The kids at school are getting used to me and Jake. At first, they all wanted to pet him, so I had to explain that when we are at school, Jake is working and can't be touched. I know Principal White had an assembly before I came back to school. Isaiah even came to talk to the kids about how to be around service dogs—no touching, no petting, but once the kids saw me with Jake, they just couldn't help themselves. They surrounded us and kept oohing and aahing. But Jake acted very professional. He didn't flinch. He just waited for me to give his command to stay. I wonder if he realizes how much he's helping me.

I spent a lot of time at the Guide Dog Center. I was in classes with Jake, learning the command words and then it was about letting Jake get used to me as his master. It's only been a few months, but I feel we are supposed to be together. Jake understands me.

I was so worried that I wouldn't be accepted back at school. Keesha told me I was wrong. Turns out she was right. The kids treat me like the same old Diana.

I see Dino from time to time. At first, Isaiah brought him over to check on us, but after a while, I caught on and realized they weren't checking on us. Isaiah wanted to spend time with Mom.

I'm really happy for her.

I'd say all of my wishes have come true.

CPSIA information can be obtained
at www.ICGtesting.com
Printed in the USA
BVHW041638300322
632853BV00016B/1289

9 781649 799951